## Legal Notice

# Roblox Meets Minecraft Diary #1

## *A Diary of Two Worlds Colliding*

Steve Robert

# Contents

Monday ................................................................8

Tuesday .............................................................16

Wednesday .......................................................40

## Monday

I don't usually change my daily routine for anyone or anything. I like the way that my life is at the moment. Stable, with things happening every day just the way that they should. My days are more or less the same all the time, and even the people who I meet don't really change.

Usually, I wake up super early and check around the house to make sure that everything looks good and is working properly. Sometimes, creatures will ruin a part of my house during the night and then I will have to fix it in the morning. But luckily, they never make too big of a mess. A few boxes go missing here and there.

I actually enjoy this part of the morning because it lets me think about life, and also gives me a few new ideas on how I can make the house look better. I always have new ideas on how to make the house more fun, but I often have to leave and to go searching for more tools to make this happen.

One of the things that I am really passionate about is having a pool. I would love to build a swimming pool for myself and to be able to swim every day whenever I want. But it isn't easy to build a pool on your own. You need to have all the tools necessary and you also need to have the patience to finish it.

It must take days of work to be able to finish a swimming pool. But, one of these days I am sure that I will be able to do it successfully and hopefully without having to ask someone else for help. It's not that I don't like working with others, it's just that I really do prefer to build things on my own.

This allows me to make them just the way I like, and I don't have to listen to anyone else's ideas. I'm sure you have guessed by now that I am not a very friendly person. But, I guess things have a way of changing when we least expect them to.

A good friend of mine over here is actually a skeleton. His name is Bob. We got to know each other after he had a bit of an accident with his own house that he was making. It turns out that he hadn't planned everything properly and had somehow started a fire in the home.

Luckily, we were able to put the fire out and he wasn't hurt, but it could have been very dangerous. That's also when we became friends. I don't think that we would have usually become friends if it was a different situation. But I guess you never know where the next day will take you.

Bob is coming over today to bring a few things. Maybe I'll tell him about the swimming pool. I wonder if he would want to build one in his own house. But then again, I am not sure how often a skeleton would actually go swimming. Probably not very often.

Either way, I am happy to have him as a friend. Bob is not someone who would do anything to disturb the way that I live. That is why I have always loved to spend time with him, even when I didn't want to play with anyone else.

13

I actually invited Bob to come over and to help me plan for everything that I had in mind to make in the house. However, neither Bob nor I were ready to start a totally new adventure so suddenly. Nothing much happens around here to be honest.

Usually, everyone just lives out their own life and sometimes we have a few fights among us. But it was never anything super serious. I guess that the arguments that sometimes happen here and there are to keep us all busy.

Oh! I can hear Bob knocking on the door right now. I'm going to let him in and to see what we can get done today. The more we do today the happier I will be tomorrow. Maybe I can even start work on my swimming pool and get it done in a few days.

## Tuesday

Yesterday started out as a normal day with Bob, but that's not how it ended. I don't think that either one of us would have correctly predicted how yesterday was going to end. I am going to walk you through the whole thing slowly so that you don't miss the shock that we had.

Bob came through the door really excited when I first saw him yesterday.

"I have good news!" said Bob. "I found some great wood on my way here which will really help with building that swimming pool that you really wanted. I know that you mentioned it a few times so I wanted to help you out, Steve."

"Oh, how nice of you!" I said. "I was just thinking about the swimming pool and I wanted to start by measuring out the area where we will build it."

"Great idea," said Bob. "Why don't we go out there right now and do it?"

So, the two of us quickly went outside and started talking about the swimming pool and where it should really go. There is a part of the garden in front of my house that I almost never use, so I was thinking of putting it there.

"How long do you think this is going to take?" I asked.

"Probably a few days," said Bob. "It will definitely take some time before it is all ready and we can put some water in it for you."

"Are you going to swim?" I asked Bob.

"No," said Bob. "But I can use one of those inflatable balloons and float around so don't worry about me."

I was very happy to hear this. After all, I really didn't want anything to happen to my friend Bob. I am glad that we came up with a plan where both of us would be able to enjoy the swimming pool.

We started by marking a big section in the garden which we would have to dig up and make the swimming pool in. However, as we were working on this, we heard a strange noise somewhere in the bushes.

"Did you hear that?" I asked Bob.

"Yes," said Bob. "I wonder what it is."

We both stopped what we were doing for a moment and we stared towards the bush where this noise was coming from. We were a little scared because we had no idea what it could be. If it was a dangerous animal, we would definitely have to run away as soon as possible.

But again, we were really not sure what was happening or why it was happening. We could just hear weird sounds coming from the bushes. Bob and I took a few steps back just in case it was something dangerous. Then, we waited for the creature to appear.

Suddenly, from the bushes came a mad. He was wearing an orange jumpsuit, and he looked really scared. We weren't sure how to react when we saw him, but he didn't seem dangerous right away. However, when he saw us looking at him he became a lot more worried.

"Who are you guys?" he asked.

"Ughh... we live around here," said Bob.

"Are the police here?" the orange guy asked.

"The police?" I asked, confused. I looked over at Bob because I had no idea what this guy was talking about.

"There's no one else here and except the two of us," said Bob. "And now you."

The orange guy looked really worried now. He looked around him, and I could tell that he didn't recognize the place where his was.

"What is this?" he asked.

"This is where we live," said Bob. "I haven't seen you around. Or anyone like you for that matter. Where did you come from?"

Now, the orange guy realized that something else was happening. I think that this is when he truly realized that something very much out of the ordinary was happening. I guess he had no idea how to handle the situation.

"What's your name?" I asked.

"Nick," said the orange guy.

"I'm Steve and this is Bob," I said. "We live in this house right here. We don't see guys like you walking around here. And why would the police be looking for you?"

Nick wasn't really ready to talk about his life at the moment. He was obviously trying to figure out what was happening to him. But honestly, I could not picture in my mind where he could have come from.

He looked around him one more time, then looked back at us. Then, he took one very serious look at Bob again, almost as if he was not used to skeletons walking around the place.

"Is this Roblox?" asked Nick.

"Roblox?" said Bob. "No, this is Minecraft."

"What's a Minecraft?" asked Nick.

"What's a Roblox?" I said.

It was now becoming more and more obvious that we are not from the same worlds. I have no idea how he managed to get here, but I had no idea if he would be able to stay or if we had to find a way to make him go back to where he came from.

"How do I go back?" asked Nick.

"How did you get here?" said Bob.

Nick thought about it for a moment. He obviously could not remember how he had made his way over here. I wondered if he would ever remember. And more importantly, what would Bob and I do with him now that he is in our lives?

"You better come inside the house," said Bob. "If the others see you they might throw a fuss before we figure out what is going on over here."

Nick agreed with Bob's idea and he quickly came inside my house. He took a seat in one of the chairs in the living room, and waited for Bob and I to start the conversation.

"Before we can help you," I said, "we need to know how you made your way all the way here. We've never seen anyone like you in this world before. Why aren't you back in your own world?"

"I had a bit of a run in with the police over in my world," said Nick. "But I didn't do it!"

"You didn't do it, but they still got you?" asked Bob.

"Yes, dude. I was in the wrong place at the wrong time, and they just grabbed me because they actually thought that I was someone else," said Nick. "It was crazy."

He looked around the house a little bit to make sure he knew where he was sitting. I wondered if he had a house of his own back home. Then, he continued.

"I really didn't want to be in prison, so I knew that I needed to find a way to escape. But I wasn't sure how to do it. Me and another guy decided to dig a hole in the ground super deep and to then dig through the prison and come out on the other side."

"That's an interesting idea," said Bob.

"Yes," said Nick. "And it actually worked. I didn't think that it would actually work but it did. But the problem was that we kept digging and digging, and suddenly we were in this weird area underground."

"A weird place underground?" I asked. "Was anyone else there with you?"

"No," said Nick. "It was just me and the other guy. It was a little scary, because we didn't know where to go to get out of it. We lost the map that we had which was showing us the way out of the ground."

"Where did you get the map from?" asked Bob.

"I don't know," said Nick. "The other guy's friend gave it to him. Then we used it to dig our way out. But we must have made a mistake somewhere along the way and that's how we ended up in that weird area. Then, a super bright light shined on us and then I don't know what happened."

"What happened to the other guy?" asked Bob.

"He disappeared," said Nick. "I don't know if he managed to get out of the prison or if he is also in some other world. Either way, we ended up getting separated."

We looked at him now with different thoughts. It was now clear to us that he was not a bad person, but instead someone who has been through a difficult time. And what is worse. He was also someone who has to run from his own world in order to feel safe.

This must have been very difficult for him to do. I cannot imagine what I would do if I had to suddenly disappear from my own home and move somewhere else. It would certainly not be easy for me to adapt to a new place. I also think that Bob feels the same way, which is probably why he wanted to help Nick, too.

"How do we get you back to your own world?" asked Bob.

"I have no idea," said Nick. "Like I said, I don't even know how I got here."

We all became silent now, as we were all trying to think of a way to help Nick to take him back home. Then, the only idea that I could possibly think of came to me. The only way for Nick to go back home, is to go back the way that he came in.

But how?

"I really do think that the only way to take you back is to literally take you back," I said. "But I am not sure how we will ever manage to actually do that."

"Exactly," said Bob. "How do we send him back if we don't know where we are sending him?"

"Do you mean that I have to dig a hole again?" asked Nick.

"Probably," I said. "It might be the only way to take you back. But who knows, maybe we will find some other way to deal with this situation. In any case, you will have to stay here for the night. There is nowhere else safe that we can send you."

Nick knew that this was the only way that we could help him, but I could also tell that he was not too happy about it. It must be very difficult for him to think about this situation right now. What if he has a family back home?

But because there was nothing else that we could possibly do to help him, I decided to prepare a special bed for him upstairs. I tried to make it as big and comfortable as possible, and I even added some colors to make it look cool. I hoped that he would use it to get a good night's sleep.

When Nick first walked into he bedroom and saw the bed, I could tell that he was very happy about it.

"Thank you, you shouldn't have," said Nick. "I really don't mean to be a bother in here. I just wanted to find a way back to my home."

"I know," I said. "And I promise that we will help you look for a way back. But the best way to do it is when it is daylight. We will not be able to achieve anything during the night, because it can become very dangerous in here."

"You're right," said Nick. "I guess we'll have to look for a proper way out tomorrow. Good night for now."

"Good night," I said. And then I left the room and let him rest until the next day.

# Wednesday

When we woke up the next morning, we had a whole new day ahead of us to try and find a way to help Nick in this difficult problem that he was in. we had a quick breakfast and then we started to plan what we were going to do that day.

It soon became clear to us that one of the first things that we would have to do is to go and walk around the area for a while to see if we could find the hole where Nick came from. The problem is that there are many different holes here, and they just appear and disappear whenever they like.

Also, there are many other creatures here who are constantly building things. We build everything here in our world in Minecraft, so it would be no wonder to us if someone had found the hole and made something new out of it. Or perhaps, the creature would disappear through the hole and into Nick's world!

"What if someone goes to your world?" asked Bob. "What would they do to him?"

"I don't think that they would do anything to them," said Nick. "But they would probably see that there is something very weird about them. Perhaps they would try to help, or perhaps they would ask them many questions."

"Especially if someone like Bob walk in, right?" I asked.

"Exactly," said Nick. "There are not exactly walking skeletons where I come from, so there would definitely be a lot of questions asked from you, my friend."

"Why does everyone always have a problem with skeletons?" asked Bob.

"Haha, calm down," I said. "At least you don't have to worry about being in another world. You are just where you need to be."

"True," said Bob.

"Well, let's get to work," I said. "We won't get anywhere if we just stay here all day and think about it."

So, we got up and made a plan. First, we needed to make sure that we change Nick's clothes. This orange outfit that he had on would definitely make him look a lot different than everyone else around him, which is why we decided to give him new clothes.

"You look similar to me," I said. "You can easily borrow some of my clothes. I really think that they will help you to fit in and to not have troubles with any of the other creatures."

So, I gave him a blur shirt and a pair of trousers which made him looks almost exactly like me. It as a little weird to look at him and sort of see myself, but it was still much better than watching him walk around looking all orange.

Next, we had to decide which part of this world we would start looking through first. The problem is that this is such a big world that it can be very difficult to find your way around if you don't know what you're doing.

Lucky for us, Bob the skeleton has been here forever and he knows almost every single corner of this place. If there was anyone who would be able to help us solve this mystery, then it would definitely be Bob and no one else.

"We're going to follow Bob's way of walking," I told Nick. "He is the only one that I trust in this place, and he will also be the only one who will actually be able to help you find your way back. Trust me, if anyone else finds you, they will look for any tools or things that you may have on you and then they will take them."

"I don't have anything on me," said Nick.

"Well, trust me," said Bob, "they will still try to search you for something interesting.

Bob was certainly not impressed to find out that the others would try and take stuff from him if they realized that he was not from these places, but I guess that he had no other choice. So instead of

worrying about it, he really tried to make the most of the situation and to come on this adventure with us.

Carefully, we left the house and took a good look around us. We wanted to make sure that the other creatures were as far away as possible, and that they would not want to come and see our guest.

"We have to be very careful from this point onwards," said Bob. "Try to be as quiet as possible, and if we do see someone who we don't want to see just ignore them. It is better than to start a confusion."

"I agree," said Nick.

So, we left the house and slowly started to walk around the place. Once we realized that no one else was there who could make the situation dangerous, we decided to keep going.

We walked for what seemed like hours. We looked behind all kinds of bushes and we jumped over tree roots. We looked into every single corner that we could think of on the way, but there was nothing that would show us that a hole had appeared somewhere.

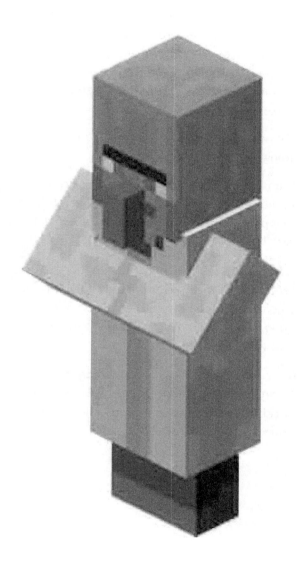

This was a big problem, because we really needed to know where the hole is in order to get Nick back into his own world. We took our time. We had no other place to be and I guess nothing else to do, except that I wanted to make a swimming pool.

"How long do you think we will need to keep going like this?" I asked Bob.

"I have no idea," said Bob. "It makes no sense to me that he ended up here in Minecraft in the first place. Do you remember how you did it, Nick?"

"No," said Nick. "The only thing that I remember is that I was definitely going through a hole. For some reason, the hole is very important. But I really don't know how I found it or why I went through it."

We continued to look for something that could be an entrance to another world. But it soon became clear to us that it is possible for the entrance to have closed.

After all, things can get really weird here in Minecraft, and it would not be weird for a portal like that to suddenly disappear. Perhaps someone else had found it before us. Or maybe it simply disappeared when the Minecraft world added its new elements, which happens every now and then.

It was getting very hot, and we were worried that we would get lost in the forest if we did not ask someone else for help. But who?

"Do we know anyone else who could help us out?" I asked Bob.

"Well," said Bob, "we sort of do, but you are not in a great relationship with him."

Then I remembered. Jack the Wizard. He is such a weirdo. Everything he does is weird, even the way he lives his life is weird. I really didn't want to talk to him at all. It's not that we got into a fight in the past, it's just that we were two very different people.

He always makes fun of the way I look, and I always make fun of the way he dresses. I don't really know when all of this started, but I knew that looking for Jack the Wizard would be a problem for me. Still, this was not about me. This was about getting Nick back to his home, which means that I had to do it.

"Alright, Bob," I said. "Do you remember where this guy lives?"

"Yes," said Bob. "He is very close by actually. If we just walk a little more we will get to him in no time."

"Well, let's go I guess," said I.

So we continued to walk forward and towards the house of Jack the Wizard. I looked back a little to check on Nick. He still seemed confused about this world that he was currently in, but at least he also looked kind of happy about hopefully finding his way back home.

After a long time of walking, we finally came in front of a house. It was a very dark and very weird looking house. Something that a wizard would definitely live in and love it. I wasn't happy about it, but I decided to be the first one to walk up to the house and ring the doorbell.

As soon as I rang the doorbell, I could hear Jack yelling from the other side.

"What are you doing here? Who are ya? Get out!" screamed Jack.

I knew that he was not happy about ever getting guests, but I also knew that he would be even less happy to see me here.

"It's me, Jack!" I yelled back. I knew that he would recognize me right away. I was kind of happy that it would make him annoyed to see me here.

"Ooooh I don't want to see you, skinny boy!" yelled Jack.

"Just open the door!" I said. "We need your help."

Just then, Jack opened the door. He looked at me, then at Bob, and then at our friend that he was definitely not expecting to see.

"Who's that?" asked Jack, pointing at Nick.

"This is our new friend," said Bob. "He just showed up here. We don't know how, but he is here. We need to get him back."

"What are you saying?" asked Jack. He was clearly confused about the whole situation. He had certainly not seen someone who did not belong to our world before.

"We're saying," I said, "that we need to find the hole that he came from. That's all we know. The only thing we know is that he came here through a hole. We've been looking for it for a long time now, but we just can't seem to find it."

"Which is why," said Bob, "we wanted to ask you if you know anything about a hole?"

Jack still looked very much confused. He looked at all of us, and then took a much closer look at Nick.  We may not be the best of friends with Jack, but we are also not enemies. We knew that there would be a way for us to figure this thing out together.

"All we ask," I said, "is that you help us to find this hole and to help us send him back. Do you think you could do that for us?"

Jack was not yet sure about whether he could do something like this or not. He then looked back at his own house.

"I didn't clean up," said Jack.

"Ughhh... we were not expecting you to," said Bob.

"All we ask," I repeated, "is that you help us find a way out of here so that we can send him back. How hard can this be?"

"Well, I supposed you better come on in then," said Jack. "I have some cookies and some drinks for you guys. We will need to talk this through first. We can't just go into the jungle and look for a hole. We have to make the hole come to us."

This all sounded so strange to us. How would he be able to make a hole come to him? How did he even know what kind of hole we were actually looking for?

But that's what a wizard does, I guess. So, with no other choice, we followed him inside the house and were looking forward to finding out what this wizard could actually do.

The wizard had a beautiful home, although it was indeed a little messy with all of the books that he had been collecting over the years. I sort of wished that he would have cleaned up a little so that we could find a place to sit down.

63

There were not many chairs, but we decided to sit on the floor anyway. Something told us that this was going to be a very long conversation. After all, who knows how long it was going to take the wizard to bring this hole to him. Hopefully not too long, because I still had a whole swimming pool to build!

"So, Jack," I said. "How long is this going to take?"

"Who knows skinny shoes," replied Jack.

Skinny shoes? What does that even mean? Jack always had the weirdest ways of making fun of me. Oh I really didn't want to be here, but there was nowhere else to go. If he couldn't help us, I really didn't know who else could do the job.

"I'm going to need a few things before we get started," said Jack.

"What do you mean?" said Nick.

"I need a few things for the potion that I am going to make. It will help to create the hole that Nick came from. Once we create the hole, you, Nick, can just go back to your own world and everything will be back to normal."

"How do you know that this is going to work?" I asked.

"Have you ever done something like this before?" asked Bob.

"No, never," said the wizard. "But I have a solution for everything that you can possibly ask me to do. After all, isn't this what wizards are for? To mysteriously help when help is needed the most?"

"I guess so," I said. "Alright, what do you need?"

Jack the wizard went to the other side of the room and picked out a few of the many books that were on the shelves on the wall. He then started to browse through them as if trying to come up with a proper plan to deal with this situation.

He looked through a few more of the books, and then he started to make something that looked like a shopping list. He made a very long list of things that he would need us to go out

66

and get. I am not sure if we would be able to do it, but there was nothing else for us to do.

When he was finished, he handed me the very piece of paper.

"Uf, this is going to be quite the adventure," I said.